A QUEER WARLD

FOUR SHORT STORIES BY JOHN BUCHAN

A Queer Warld

FOUR SHORT STORIES

BY JOHN BUCHAN

THE HERD OF STANDLAN

ON CADEMUIR HILL

AT THE RISING OF THE WATERS

SKULE SKERRY

Introduction by Robert Hume

Published by
Association for Scottish Literature
Scottish Literature
7 University Gardens
University of Glasgow
Glasgow G12 8QH

www.asls.org.uk

ASL is a registered charity no. SC006535

"The Herd of Standlan" (published in *Grey Weather*, 1899)

"On Cademuir Hill" (published in *Scholar Gipsies*, 1896)

"At the Rising of the Waters" (published in *Grey Weather*, 1899)

"Skule Skerry" (published in *The Runagates Club*, 1928)

This edition published 2024
Typeset by ASL in Adobe Caslon Pro

Cover image by Patrimonio Designs (Adobe Stock)

Introduction © Robert Hume 2024

ISBN 978-1-906841-62-1

ASL acknowledges the support of the Scottish Government
towards the publication of this book

Printed by Ashford Colour Press, Gosport

CONTENTS

Introduction . . . . *vii*

The Herd of Standlan 1

On Cademuir Hill 17

At the Rising of the Waters 25

Skule Skerry 37

Glossary 57

INTRODUCTION

Robert Hume

Even the briefest glance at John Buchan's biography would provoke a sense of wonder at such a full life: born in 1875 (therefore, truly a Victorian); a son of the manse, but one from penurious circumstances; winner of a scholarship, leading to a brilliant First at Oxford, but failure to gain a prized Fellowship; followed by coming to the Bar, making his way in London society, and editing *The Spectator*. Then work in public service, firstly in South Africa, initially serving under Viscount Milner (the most famous, yet contentious of the great Victorian colonial administrators of the Empire) in the necessary reconstruction following the Boer War, then, following rejection for military service in 1914 on age and health grounds, work with Military Intelligence and Propaganda, followed by service as an MP in the 1920s and 30s. Then, lastly and most famously, in Canada as Governor General. Truly a lad o pairts.

Yet at the same time as he was making his way through this busy public life, Buchan was also embarking on a writing career which produced ninety publications: not just the famous

Hannay novels which he called his 'shockers', but a range of other novels across a variety of genres (from the historical to the thriller to the comic to the occult), short stories, journalism in his involvement with *The Spectator*, history and biography; and not forgetting his role in helping set up the British Film Institute and getting to know Alfred Hitchcock, leading to the famous 1935 film version of *The Thirty-Nine Steps*, so responsible for his popular success. And in this career he associated with generations of famous literary figures, from his contributions to Aubrey Beardsley's *The Yellow Book* to his friendships with T. E. Lawrence, Virginia Woolf, Hugh MacDiarmid and Ezra Pound.

All of this while having to overcome a number of life's blows. He endured several health problems: from the fractured skull suffered in a childhood accident, and the extended convalescence afterwards; to the years increasingly debilitated by a duodenal ulcer, then seen as an incurable condition. And a personal life devastated by the First World War, which led to the deaths of so many of his family and close friends from his Oxford days. And, finally, the fatal accidental fall leading to his death on the 11th of February 1940. It is also probably true that his modest assessment of his own abilities (he described his writing as 'high-lowbrow') combined with the sheer breadth of his activities gave rise to the criticism that he 'spread himself too thin'; and, over time, some diminishing in critical esteem. Yet for all the features which establish him as a man of his times, in his fiction he consistently addresses a number of profound issues, many of which are still of lively concern nowadays.

This selection mostly concentrates on his earlier short stories, with their focus on the landscape he came to know while growing up in the farmland around Peebles and the Borders. Yet even in his earliest work (and 'On Cademuir Hill' is his earliest published piece), he displays the technical mastery of writing which would become a trademark, and an awareness of a sense of place, and the characters it bred. The choice of these short stories also illustrates both a 'Scottish voice' and an 'English voice', and his obvious skill with both. And though they are longer than is the present fashion, it is hoped their brevity will help to introduce his writing to a new generation of readers.

> 'John Buchan's combination of unusual direct experience of landscape and a quite remarkable literary use of word patterns gives his writing extraordinary force.'
> —David Daniell, *The Interpreter's House: A Critical Assessment of John Buchan*

> 'We have all our own Scotlands . . .'
> —John Buchan, *The Gap in the Curtain*

Robert Hume
Spring / Summer 2024

THE HERD OF STANDLAN

"When the wind is nigh and the moon is high
    And the mist on the riverside,
Let such as fare have a very good care
    Of the Folk who come to ride.
For they may meet with the riders fleet
    Who fare from the place of dread;
And hard it is for a mortal man
    To sort at ease with the Dead."

The Ballad of Grey Weather.

WHEN STANDLAN BURN leaves the mosses and hags which gave it birth, it tumbles over a succession of falls into a deep, precipitous glen, whence in time it issues into a land of level green meadows, and finally finds its rest in the Gled. Just at the opening of the ravine there is a pool shut in by high, dark cliffs, and black even on the most sunshiny day. The rocks are never dry but always black with damp and shadow. There is scarce any vegetation save stunted birks, juniper bushes, and draggled fern; and the hoot of owls and the croak of hooded crows is seldom absent from the spot. It is the famous Black Linn where in winter sheep stray and are never more heard of, and where more than once an unwary shepherd has gone to his account. It is an Inferno on the brink of a Paradise, for not a stone's throw off is the green, lawn-like turf, the hazel thicket, and the broad, clear pools, by the edge of which on that July day the Herd of Standlan and I sat drowsily smoking and talking of fishing and the hills. There he told me this story, which I here set down as I remember it, and as it bears repetition.

"D'ye mind Airthur Morrant?" said the shepherd, suddenly.

I did remember Arthur Mordaunt. Ten years past he and I had been inseparables, despite some half-dozen summers difference in age. We had fished and shot together, and together we had tramped every hill within thirty miles. He had come up from the South to try sheep-farming, and as he came of a great family and had no need to earn his bread, he found the profession pleasing. Then irresistible fate had swept me southward to college, and when after two years I came back to the place, his father was dead and he had come into his own. The next I heard of him was that in politics he was regarded as the most promising of the younger men, one of the staunchest and ablest upstays of the Constitution. His name was rapidly rising into prominence, for he seemed to exhibit that rare phenomenon of a man of birth and culture in direct sympathy with the wants of the people.

"You mean Lord Brodakers?" said I.

"Dinna call him by that name," said the shepherd, darkly. "I hae nae thocht o' him now. He's a disgrace to his country, servin' the Deil wi' baith hands. But nine year syne he was a bit innocent callant wi' nae Tory deevilry in his heid. Well, as I was sayin', Airthur Morrant has cause to mind that place till his dying day;" and he pointed his finger to the Black Linn.

I looked up the chasm. The treacherous water, so bright and joyful at our feet, was like ink in the great gorge. The swish and plunge of the cataract came like the regular beating of a clock, and though the weather was dry, streams of moisture seamed the perpendicular walls. It was a place eerie even on that bright summer's day.

"I don't think I ever heard the story," I said casually.

"Maybe no," said the shepherd. "It's no yin I like to tell;" and he puffed sternly at his pipe, while I awaited the continuation.

"Ye see it was like this," he said, after a while. "It was just the beginning o' the back end, and that year we had an awfu' spate o' rain. For near a week it poured hale water, and a' doon by Drumeller and the Mossfennan haughs was yae muckle loch. Then it stopped, and an awfu' heat came on. It dried the grund in nae time, but it hardly touched the burns; and it was rale queer to be pourin' wi' sweat and the grund aneath ye as dry as a potato-sack, and a' the time the water neither to haud nor bind. A' the waterside fields were clean stripped o' stooks, and a guid wheen hay-ricks gaed doon tae Berwick, no to speak o' sheep and nowt beast. But that's anither thing.

"Weel, ye'll mind that Airthur was terrible keen on the fishing. He wad gang oot in a' weather, and he wasna feared for ony mortal or naitural thing. Dod, I've seen him in Gled wi' the water rinnin' ower his shouthers yae cauld March day playin' a saumon. He kenned weel aboot the fishing, for he had traivelled in Norroway and siccan outlandish places, where there's a heap o' big fish. So that day—and it was a Setterday tae and far ower near the Sabbath—he maun gang awa' up Standlan Burn wi' his rod and creel to try his luck.

"I was bidin' at that time, as ye mind, in the wee cot-house at the back o' the faulds. I was alane, for it was three year afore I mairried Jess, and I wasna begun yet to the coortin'. I had been at Gledsmuir that day for some o' the new stuff for killing sheep-mawks, and I wasna very fresh on my legs when I gaed oot after my tea that nicht to hae a look at the hill-sheep. I had had a bad year on the hill. First the lambin'-time was snaw, snaw ilka day, and I lost mair than I wad like to tell. Syne the grass a' summer was so short wi' the drought that the puir beasts could scarcely get a bite and were as thin as pipe-stapples. And then, to crown a', auld Will Broun, the man that helpit me, turned ill wi' his back, and had to bide at hame. So I had twae man's wark on yae man's shouthers, and was nane so weel pleased.

"As I was saying, I gaed oot that nicht, and after lookin' a' the Dun Rig and the Yellow Mire and the back o' Cramalt Craig, I cam down the burn by the road frae the auld faulds. It was geyan dark, being about seven o'clock o' a September nicht, and I keepit weel back frae that wanchancy hole o' a burn. Weel, I was comin' kind o' quick, thinkin' o' supper and a story-book that I was readin' at the time, when just abune that place there, at the foot o' the Linn, I saw a man fishing. I wondered what ony body in his senses could be daein' at that time o' nicht in sic a dangerous place, so I gave him a roar and bade him come back. He turned his face round and I saw in a jiffey that it was Mr Airthur.

"'O, sir,' I cried, 'what for are ye fishing there? The water's awfu' dangerous, and the rocks are far ower slid.'

"'Never mind, Scott,' he roars back cheery-like. 'I'll take care o' mysel'.'

"I lookit at him for twa-three meenutes, and then I saw by his rod he had yin on, and a big yin tae. He ran it up and doon the pool, and he had uncommon wark wi' 't, for it was strong and there was little licht. But bye and bye he got it almost tae his feet, and was just about to lift it oot when a maist awfu' thing happened. The tackets o' his boots maun hae slithered on the stane, for the next thing I saw was Mr Airthur in the muckle hungry water.

"I dinna exactly ken what happened after that, till I found myself on the very stone he had slipped off. I maun hae come doon the face o' the rocks, a thing I can scarcely believe when I look at them, and a thing no man ever did afore. At ony rate I ken I fell the last fifteen feet or sae, and lichted on my left airm, for I felt it crack like a rotten branch, and an awfu' sairness ran up it.

"Now, the pool is a whirlpool as ye ken, and if anything fa's in, the water first smashes it against the muckle rock at the foot, then it brings it round below the fall again, and syne at the second time it carries it doon the burn. Weel, that was what happened to Mr Airthur. I heard his heid gang dunt on the stane wi' a sound that made me sick. This must hae dung him clean senseless, and indeed it was a wonder it didna knock his brains oot. At ony rate there was nae mair word o' swimming, and he was swirled round below the fa' just like a corp.

"I kenned fine that nae time was to be lost, for if he once gaed doun the burn he wad be in Gled or ever I could say a word, and nae man wad ever see him mair in life. So doon I got on my hunkers on the stane, and waited for the turnin'. Round he came, whirling in the foam, wi' a lang line o' blood across his brow where the stane had cut him. It was a terrible meenute. My heart fair stood still. I put out my airm, and as he passed I grippit him and wi' an awfu' pu' got him out o' the current into the side.

"But now I found that a waur thing still was on me. My left airm was broken, and my richt sae numbed and weak wi' my fall that, try as I micht, I couldna raise him ony further. I thocht I wad burst a blood-vessel i' my face and my muscles fair cracked wi' the strain, but I could make nothing o' 't. There he stuck wi' his heid and shouthers abune the water, pu'd close until the edge of a rock.

"What was I to dae? If I once let him slip he wad be into the stream and lost forever. But I couldna hang on here a' nicht, and as far as I could see there wad be naebody near till the mornin', when Ebie Blackstock passed frae the Head o' the Hope. I roared wi' a' my power; but I got nae answer, naething but the rummle o' the water and the whistling o' some whaups on the hill.

"Then I turned very sick wi' terror and pain and weakness and I kenna what. My broken airm seemed a great lump o' burnin' coal. I maun hae given it some extra wrench when I hauled him out, for it was sae sair now that I thocht I could scarcely thole it. Forbye, pain and a', I could hae gone off to sleep wi' fair weariness. I had heard tell o' men sleepin' on their feet, but I never felt it till then. Man, if I hadna warstled wi' mysel, I wad hae dropped off as deid's a peery.

"Then there was the awfu' strain o' keepin' Mr Airthur up. He was a great big man, twelve stone I'll warrant, and weighing a terrible lot mair wi' his fishing togs and things. If I had had the use o' my ither airm I micht hae taen off his jacket and creel and lichtened the burden, but I could do naething. I scarcely like to tell ye how I was tempted in that hour. Again and again I says to mysel, 'Gidden Scott,' says I, 'what do ye care for this man? He's no a drap's bluid to you, and forbye ye'll never be able to save him. Ye micht as weel let him gang. Ye've dune a' ye could. Ye're a brave man, Gidden Scott, and ye've nae cause to be ashamed o' givin' up the fecht.' But I says to mysel again: 'Gidden Scott, ye're a coward. Wad ye let a man die, when there's a breath in your body? Think shame o' yoursel, man.' So I aye kept haudin' on, although I was very near bye wi' 't. Whenever I lookit at Mr Airthur's face, as white's death and a' blood, and his een sae stelled-like, I got a kind o' groo and felt awfu' pitiful for the bit laddie. Then I thocht on his faither, the auld Lord, wha was sae built up in him, and I couldna bear to think o' his son droonin' in that awfu' hole. So I set mysel to the wark o' keepin' him up a' nicht, though I had nae hope in the matter. It wasna what ye ca' bravery that made me dae't, for I had nae ither choice. It was just a kind o' dourness that runs in my folk, and a kind o' vexedness for sae young a callant in sic an ill place.

"The nicht was hot and there was scarcely a sound o' wind. I felt the sweat standin' on my face like frost on tatties, and abune me the sky was a' misty and nae mune visible. I thocht very likely that it micht come a thunder shower and I kind o' lookit forrit tae 't. For I was aye feared at lichtning, and if it came that nicht I was bound to get clean dazed and likely tummle in. I was a lonely man wi' nae kin to speak o', so it wouldna maitter muckle.

"But now I come to tell ye about the queer side o' that nicht's wark, whilk I never telled to nane but yoursel, though a' the folk about here ken the rest. I maun hae been geyan weak, for I got into a kind o' doze, no sleepin', ye understand, but awfu' like it. And then a' sort o' daft things began to dance afore my een. Witches and bogles and brownies and things oot o' the Bible, and leviathans and brazen bulls—a' cam fleerin' and flauntin' on the tap o' the water straucht afore me. I didna pay muckle heed to them, for I half kenned it was a' nonsense, and syne they gaed awa'. Then an auld wife wi' a mutch and a hale procession o' auld wives passed, and just about the last I saw yin I thocht I kenned.

"'Is that you, grannie?' says I.

"'Ay, it's me, Gidden,' says she; and as shure as I'm a leevin' man, it was my auld grannie, whae had been deid thae sax year. She had on the same mutch as she aye wore, and the same auld black stickie in her hand, and, Dod, she had the same snuff-box I made for her out o' a sheep's horn when I first took to the herdin'. I thocht she was lookin' rale weel.

"'Losh, Grannie,' says I, 'where in the warld hae ye come frae? It's no canny to see ye danderin' about there.'

"'Ye've been badly brocht up,' she says, 'and ye ken nocht about it. Is't no a decent and comely thing that I should get a breath o' air yince in the while?'

"'Deed,' said I, 'I had forgotten. Ye were sae like yoursel I never had a mind ye were deid. And how d' ye like the Guid Place?'

"'Wheesht, Gidden,' says she, very solemn-like, 'I'm no there.'

"Now at this I was fair flabbergasted. Grannie had aye been a guid contentit auld wumman, and to think that they hadna let her intil Heeven made me think ill o' my ain chances.

"'Help us, ye dinna mean to tell me ye're in Hell?' I cries.

"'No exactly,' says she, 'but I'll trouble ye, Gidden, to speak mair respectful about holy things. That's a name ye uttered the noo whilk we dinna daur to mention.'

"'I'm sorry, Grannie,' says I, 'but ye maun allow it's an astonishin' thing for me to hear. We aye counted ye shure, and ye died wi' the Buik in your hands.'

"'Weel,' she says, 'it was like this. When I gaed up till the gate o' Heeven a man wi' a lang white robe comes and says, "Wha may ye be?" Says I, "I'm Elspeth Scott." He gangs awa' and consults a wee and then he says, "I think, Elspeth my wumman, ye'll hae to gang doon the brae a bit. Ye're no quite guid eneuch for this place, but ye'll get a very comfortable doonsittin' whaur I tell ye." So off I gaed and cam' to a place whaur the air was like the inside of the glass-houses at the Lodge. They took me in wi'oot a word and I've been rale comfortable. Ye see they keep the bad part o' the Ill Place for the reg'lar bad folk, but they've a very nice half-way house where the likes o' me stop.'

"'And what kind o' company hae ye?'

"'No very select,' says she. 'There's maist o' the ministers o' the countryside and a' pickle fairmers, tho' the maist o' them are further ben. But there's my son Jock, your ain faither, Gidden, and a heap o' folk from the village, and oh, I'm nane sae bad.'

"'Is there naething mair ye wad like then, Grannie?'

"'Oh aye,' says she, 'we've each yae thing which we canna get. It's a' the punishment we hae. Mine's butter. I canna get fresh butter for my bread, for ye see it winna keep, it just melts. So I've to tak jeely to ilka slice, whilk is rale sair on the teeth. Ye'll no hae ony wi' ye?'

"'No,' I says, 'I've naething but some tobaccy. D'ye want it? Ye were aye fond o' 't.'

"'Na, na,' says she. 'I get plenty o' tobbaccy doon bye. The pipe's never out o' the folks' mouth there. But I'm no speakin' about yoursel, Gidden. Ye're in a geyan ticht place.'

"'I'm a' that,' I said. 'Can ye no help me?'

"'I micht try.' And she raxes out her hand to grip mine. I put out mine to tak it, never thinkin' that that wasna the richt side, and that if Grannie grippit it she wad pu' the broken airm and haul me into the water. Something touched my fingers like a hot poker; I gave a great yell; and ere ever I kenned I was awake, a' but off the rock, wi' my left airm aching like hell-fire. Mr Airthur I had let slunge ower the heid and my ain legs were in the water.

"I gae an awfu' whammle and edged my way back though it was near bye my strength. And now anither thing happened. For the cauld water roused Mr Airthur frae his dwam. His een opened and he gave a wild look around him. 'Where am I?' he cries, 'O God!' and he gaed off intil anither faint.

"I can tell ye, sir, I never felt anything in this warld and I hope never to feel anything in anither sae bad as the next meenutes on that rock. I was fair sick wi' pain and weariness and a kind o' fever. The lip-lap o' the water, curling round Mr Airthur, and the great *crush* o' the Black Linn itsel dang me fair silly. Then there was my airm, which was bad eneuch, and abune a' I was gotten into sic a state that I was fleyed at ilka shadow just like a bairn. I felt fine I was gaun daft, and if the thing had lasted anither score o' meenutes I wad be in a madhouse this day. But soon I felt the sleepiness comin' back, and I was off again dozin' and dreamin'.

"This time it was nae auld wumman but a muckle black-avised man that was standin' in the water glowrin' at me. I kenned him fine by the bandy-legs o' him and the broken nose (whilk I did mysel), for Dan Kyle the poacher deid thae twae year. He was a man, as I remembered him weel, wi' a great black beard and een that were stuck sae far in his heid that they looked like twae wull-cats keekin' oot o' a hole. He stands and just stares at me, and never speaks a word.

"'What d' ye want?' I yells, for by this time I had lost a' grip o' mysel. 'Speak, man, and dinna stand there like a dummy.'

"'I want naething,' he says in a mournfu' sing-song voice; 'I'm just thinkin'.'

"'Whaur d' ye come frae?' I asked, 'and are ye keepin' weel?'

"'Weel,' he says bitterly. 'In this warld I was ill to my wife, and twa-three times I near killed a man, and I stole like a pyet, and I was never sober. How d' ye think I should be weel in the next?'

"I was sorry for the man. 'D' ye ken I'm vexed for ye, Dan,' says I; 'I never likit ye when ye were here, but I'm wae to think ye're sae ill off yonder.'

"'I'm no alane,' he says. 'There's Mistress Courhope o' the Big House, she's waur. Ye mind she was awfu' fond o' gum-flowers. Weel, she canna keep them Yonder, for they a' melt wi' the heat. She's in an ill way about it, puir body.' Then he broke off. 'Whae's that ye've got there? Is't Airthur Morrant?'

"'Ay, it's Airthur Morrant,' I said.

"'His family's weel kent doon bye,' says he. 'We've maist o' his forbears, and we're expectin' the auld Lord every day. May be we'll sune get the lad himsel.'

"'That's a damned lee,' says I, for I was angry at the man's presumption.

"Dan lookit at me sorrowfu'-like. 'We'll be gettin' you tae, if ye swear that gate,' says he, 'and then ye'll ken what it's like.'

"Of a sudden I fell into a great fear. 'Dinna say that, Dan,' I cried; 'I'm better than ye think. I'm a deacon, and 'll maybe sune be an elder, and I never swear except at my dowg.'

"'Tak care, Gidden,' said the face afore me. 'Where I am, a' things are taken into account.'

"'Then they'll hae a gey big account for you,' says I. 'What-like do they treat you, may be?'

"The man groaned.

"'I'll tell ye what they dae to ye doon there,' he said. 'They put ye intil a place a' paved wi' stanes and wi' four square walls around. And there's naething in 't, nae grass, nae shadow. And abune you there's a sky like brass. And sune ye get terrible hot and thirsty, and your tongue sticks to your mouth, and your eyes get blind wi' lookin' on the white stane. Then ye gang clean fey, and dad your heid on the ground and the walls to try and kill yoursel. But though ye dae 't till a' eternity ye couldna feel pain. A' that ye feel is just the awfu' devourin' thirst, and the heat and the weariness. And if ye lie doon the ground burns ye and ye're fain to get up. And ye canna lean on the walls for the heat, and bye and bye when ye're fair perished wi' the thing, they tak ye out to try some ither ploy.'

"'Nae mair,' I cried, 'nae mair, Dan!'

"But he went on malicious-like,—'Na, na, Gidden, I'm no dune yet. Syne they tak you to a fine room but awfu' warm. And there's a big fire in the grate and thick woollen rugs on the floor. And in the corner there's a braw feather bed. And they lay ye down on't, and then they pile on the tap o' ye mattresses and blankets and sacks and great rolls o' woollen stuff miles wide. And then ye see what they're after, tryin' to suffocate ye as they dae to folk that a mad dowg has bitten. And ye try to kick them off, but they're ower heavy, and ye canna move your feet nor your airms nor gee your heid. Then ye gang clean gyte and skirl to yoursel, but your voice is choked and naebody is near. And the warst o' 't is that ye canna die and get it ower. It's like death a hundred times and yet ye're aye leevin'. Bye and bye when they think ye've got eneuch they tak you out and put ye somewhere else.'

"'Oh,' I cries, 'stop, man, or you'll ding me silly.'

"But he says never a word, just glowrin' at me.

"'Aye, Gidden, and waur than that. For they put ye in a great loch wi' big waves just like the sea at the Pier o' Leith. And there's nae chance o' soomin', for as sune as ye put out your airms a billow gulfs ye down. Then ye swallow water and your heid dozes round and ye're chokin'. But ye canna die, ye must just thole. And down ye gang, down, down, in the cruel deep, till your heid's like to burst and your een are fu' o' bluid. And there's a' kind o' fearfu' monsters about, muckle slimy things wi' blind een and white scales, that claw at ye wi' claws just like the paws o' a drooned dog. And ye canna get away though ye fecht and fleech, and bye and bye ye're fair mad wi' horror and choking and the feel o' thae awfu' things. Then—'

"But now I think something snapped in my heid, and I went daft in doonricht earnest. The man before me danced about like a lantern's shine on a windy nicht and then disappeared. And I woke yelling like a pig at a killing, fair wud wi' terror, and my skellochs made the rocks ring. I found mysel in the pool a' but yae airm—the broken yin—which had hankit in a crack o' rock. Nae wonder I had been dreaming o' deep waters among the torments o' the Ill Place, when I was in them mysel. The pain in my airm was sae fearsome and my heid was gaun round sae wi' horror that I just skirled on and on, shrieking and groaning wi'oot a thocht what I was daein'. I was as near death as ever I will be, and as for Mr Airthur he was on the very nick o' 't, for by this time he was a' in the water, though I still kept a grip o' him.

"When I think ower it often I wonder how it was possible that I could be here the day. But the Lord's very gracious, and he works in a queer way. For it so happened that Ebie Blackstock, whae had left Gledsmuir an hour afore me and whom I thocht by this time to be snorin' in his bed at the Head o' the Hope, had gone intil the herd's house at the Waterfit, and had got sae muckle drink there that he was sweered to start for hame till aboot half-past twal i' the night. Weel, he was comin' up the burnside, gae happy and contentit, for he had nae wife at hame to speir about his ongaeings, when, as he's telled me himsel, he heard sic an uproar doon by the Black Linn that made him turn pale and think that the Deil, whom he had long served, had gotten him at last. But he was a brave man, was Ebie, and he thinks to himsel that some fellow-creature micht be perishin'. So he gangs forrit wi' a' his pith, trying to think on the Lord's Prayer and last Sabbath's sermon. And, lookin' ower the edge, he saw naething for a while, naething but the black water wi' the awfu' yells coming out o' 't. Then he made out something like a heid near the side. So he rins doon by the road, no ower the rocks as I had come, but round by the burnside road, and soon he gets to the pool, where the crying was getting aye fainter and fainter. And then he saw me. And he grips me by the collar, for he was a sensible man, was Ebie, and hauls me oot. If he hadna been geyan strong he couldna hae dune it, for I was a deid wecht, forbye having a heavy man hanging on to me. When he got me up, what was his astonishment to find anither man at the end o' my airm, a man like a corp a' bloody about the heid. So he got us baith out, and we wae baith senseless; and he laid us in a safe bit back frae the water, and syne gaed off for help. So bye and bye we were baith got hame, me to my house and Mr Airthur up to the Lodge."

"And was that the end of it?" I asked.

"Na," said the shepherd. "I lay for twae month there raving wi' brain fever, and when I cam to my senses I was as weak as a bairn. It was many months ere I was mysel again, and my left airm to this day is stiff and no muckle to lippen to. But Mr Airthur was far waur, for the dad he had gotten on the rock was thocht to have broken his skull, and he lay long atween life and death. And the warst thing was that his faither was sae vexed about him that he never got ower the shock, but dee'd afore Airthur was out o' bed. And so when he cam out again he was My Lord, and a monstrously rich man."

The shepherd puffed meditatively at his pipe for a few minutes.

"But that's no a' yet. For Mr Airthur wad tak nae refusal but that I maun gang awa' doon wi' him to his braw house in England and be a land o' factor or steward or something like that. And I had a rale fine cottage a' to mysel, wi' a very bonny gairden and guid wages, so I stayed there maybe sax month and then I gaed up till him. 'I canna bide nae longer,' says I. 'I canna stand this place. It's far ower laigh, and I'm fair sick to get hills to rest my een on. I'm awfu' gratefu' to ye for your kindness, but I maun gie up my job.' He was very sorry to lose me, and was for gien' me a present o' money or stockin' a fairm for me, because he said that it was to me he owed his life. But I wad hae nane o' his gifts. 'It wad be a terrible thing,' I says, 'to tak siller for daein' what ony body wad hae dune out o' pity.' So I cam awa' back to Standlan, and I maun say I'm rale contentit here. Mr Airthur used whiles to write to me and ca' in and see me when he cam North for the shooting; but since he's gane sae far wrang wi' the Tories, I've had naething mair to dae wi' him."

I made no answer, being busy pondering in my mind on the depth of the shepherd's political principles, before which the ties of friendship were as nothing.

"Ay," said he, standing up, "I did what I thocht my duty at the time and I was rale glad I saved the callant's life. But now, when I think on a' the ill he's daein' to the country and the Guid Cause, I whiles think I wad hae been daein' better if I had just drappit him in.

"But whae kens? It's a queer warld." And the shepherd knocked the ashes out of his pipe.

ON CADEMUIR HILL

I

THE GAMEKEEPER OF Cademuir strode in leisurely fashion over the green side of the hill. The bright chilly morning was past, and the heat had all but begun; but he had lain long a-bed, deeming that life was too short at the best, and there was little need to hurry it over. He was a man of a bold carriage, with the indescribable air of one whose life is connected with sport and rough moors. A steady grey eye and a clean chin were his best features; otherwise, he was of the ordinary make of a man, looking like one born for neither good nor evil in any high degree. The sunlight danced around him, and flickered among the brackens; and though it was an everyday sight with him, he was pleased, and felt cheerful, just like any wild animal on a bright day. If he had had his dog with him, he would have sworn at it to show his pleasure; as it was, he contented himself with whistling "The Linton Ploughman", and setting his heels deep into the soft green moss.

The day was early and his way was long, for he purposed to go up Manor Water to the shepherd's house about a matter of some foxes. It might be ten miles, it might be more; and the keeper was in no great haste, for there was abundant time to get his dinner and a smoke with the herd, and then come back in the cool of the evening; for it was summer-time, when men of his class have their holiday. Two miles more, and he would strike the highway; he could see it even now coiling beneath the straight sides of the glen. There it was easy walking, and he would get on quickly; but now he might take his time. So he lit his pipe, and looked complacently around him.

At the turn of the hill, where a strip of wood runs up the slope, he stopped, and a dark shadow came over his face. This was the place where, not two weeks ago, he had chased a poacher, and but for the fellow's skill in doubling, would have caught him. He cursed the whole tribe in his heart. They were the bane of his easy life. They came at night, and took him out on the bleak hillside when he should have been in his bed. They might have a trap there even now. He would go and see, for it was not two hundred yards from his path.

So he climbed up the little howe in the hill beside the firwood, where the long thickets of rushes, and the rabbit-warrens made a happy hunting-ground for the enemies of the law. A snipe or two flew up as he approached, and a legion of rabbits scurried into their holes. He had all but given up the quest, when the gleam of something among the long grass caught his attention, and in a trice he had pulled back the herbage, and disclosed a neatly set and well-constructed trap.

It was a very admirable trap. He had never seen one like it; so in a sort of angry exultation, as he thought of how he would spoil this fine game, he knelt down to examine it. It was no mere running noose, but of strong steel, and firmly fixed to the trunk of an old tree. No unhappy pheasant would ever move it, were its feet once caught in its strong teeth. He felt the iron with his hand, feeling down the sides for the spring; when suddenly with a horrid snap the thing closed on him, pinning his hand below the mid-finger, and he was powerless.

The pain was terrible, agonising. His hand burned like white fire, and every nerve of his body tingled. With his left hand he attempted to loosen it, but the spring was so well concealed, that he could not find it. Perhaps, too, he may have lost his wits, for in any great suffering the brain is seldom clear. After a few minutes of feeble searching and tugging, every motion of which gave agony to his imprisoned hand, he gave it up, and, in something very like panic, sought for his knife to try to cut the trap loose from the trunk. And now a fresh terror awaited him, for he found that he had no knife; he had left it in another coat, which was in his room at home. With a sigh of infinite pain, he stopped the search, and stared drearily before him.

He confusedly considered his position. He was fixed with no possibility of escape, some two miles from the track of any chance passer-by. They would not look for him at home until the evening, and the shepherd at Manor did not know of his coming. Some one might be on the hill, but then this howe was on a remote side where few ever came, unless their duty brought them. Below him in the valley was the road with some white cottages beside it. There were women in those houses, living and moving not far from him; they might see him if he were to wave something as a signal. But then, he reflected with a groan, that though he could see their dwellings, they could not see him, for he was hidden by the shoulder of the hill.

Once more he made one frantic effort to escape, but it was unsuccessful. Then he leant back upon the heather, gnawing his lips to help him to endure the agony of the wound. He was a strong man, broad and sinewy, and where a weaker might have swooned, he was left to endure the burden of a painful consciousness. Again he thought of escape. The man who had set the trap must come to see it, but it might not be that day, nor the next. He pictured his friends hunting up and down Manor Water, every pool and wood; passing and re-passing not two hundred yards from where he was lying dead, or worse than dead. His mind grew sick at the thought, and he had almost fainted in spite of his strength.

Then he fell into a panic, the terror of rough "hard-handed men, which never laboured in their mind." His brain whirled, his eyes were stelled, and a shiver shook him like a reed. He puzzled over his past life, feeling, in a dim way, that it had not been as it should be. He had been drunk often, he had not been over-careful of the name of the Almighty; was not this some sort of retribution? He strove to pray, but he could think of no words. He had been at church last Sunday, and he tried to think of what he had heard; but try as he would, nothing came to his mind, but the chorus of a drinking-song he had often heard sung in the public-house at Peebles:

> When the hoose is rinnin' round about,
>   It's time eneuch to flit;
> For we've lippened aye to Providence,
>   And sae will we yet.

The irony of the words did not strike him; but fervently, feverishly, he repeated them, as if for the price of his soul.

The fit passed, and a wild frenzy of rage took him. He cursed like a fiend, and yelled horrible menaces upon the still air. If he had the man who set this trap, he would strangle the life out of him here on this spot. No, that was too merciful. He would force his arm into the trap, and take him to some lonely place where never a human being came from one year's end to the other. Then he would let him die, and come to gloat over his suffering. With every turn of his body he wrenched his hand, and with every wrench, he yelled more madly, till he lay back exhausted, and the green hills were left again in peace.

Then he slept a sleep which was half a swoon, for maybe an hour, though to him it seemed like ages. He seemed to be dead, and in torment; and the place of his torment was this same hillside. On the brae face, a thousand evil spirits were mocking his anguish, and not only his hand, but his whole body was imprisoned in a remorseless trap. He felt the keen steel crush through his bones, like a spade through a frosted turnip. He woke screaming with nameless dread, looking on every side for the infernal faces of his dreams, but seeing nothing but a little chaffinch hopping across the turf.

Then came for him a long period of slow, despairing agony. The hot air glowed, and the fierce sun beat upon his face. A thousand insects hummed about him, bees and butterflies and little hill-moths. The wholesome smell of thyme and bent was all about him, and every now and then a little breeze broke the stillness, and sent a ripple over the grass. The genial warmth seemed stifling; his head ached, and his breath came in sudden gasps. An overpowering thirst came upon him, and his tongue was like a burnt stick in his mouth. Not ten feet off, a little burn danced over a minute cascade. He could see the dust of spray, which wet the cool green rushes. The pleasant tinkle sang in his ears, and mocked his fever. He tried to think of snow and ice and cold water, but his brain refused to do its part, and he could get nothing but an intolerable void.

Far across the valley, the great forehead of Dollar Law raised itself, austere and lofty. To his unquiet sight, it seemed as if it rolled over on Scrape, and the two played pranks among the lower hills beyond. The idea came to him, how singularly unpleasant it would be for the people there—among them a shepherd to whom he owed two pounds. He would be crushed to powder, and there would be no more of the debt at any rate. Then a text from the Scriptures came to haunt him, something, he could scarce tell exactly, about the hills and mountains leaping like rams. Here it was realised before his very eyes. Below him, in the peaceful valley, Manor Water seemed to be wrinkled across it, like a scrawl from the pen of a bad writer. When a bird flew past, or a hare started from its form, he screamed with terror, and all the wholesome sights of a summer day were wrought by his frenzied brain into terrible phantoms. So true is it that Natura Benigna and Natura Maligna may walk hand in hand upon the same hillside.

Then came the time when the strings of the reason are all but snapped, and a man becomes maudlin. He thought of his young wife, not six weeks married, and grieved over her approaching sorrow. He wept unnatural tears, which, if any one had been there to see him, would have been far more terrible than his frantic ravings. He pictured to himself in gruesome detail, the finding of his body, how his wife would sob, and his friends would shake their heads, and swear that he had been an honest fellow, and that it was a pity that he was away. The place would soon forget him; his wife would marry again; his dogs would get a new master, and he—

ay, that was the question, where would he be? and a new dread took him, as he thought of the fate which might await him. The unlettered man, in his times of dire necessity, has nothing to go back upon but a mind full of vivid traditions, which are the most merciless of things.

It might be about three or four o'clock but by the clock in his brain it was weeks later, that he suffered that supremacy of pain, which any one who has met it once, would walk to the end of the earth to avoid. The world shrank away from him; his wits forsook him; and he cried out, till the lonely rocks rang, and the whaups mingled their startled cries with his. With a last effort, he crushed down his head with his unwounded hand upon the tree-trunk, till blessed unconsciousness took him into her merciful embrace.

II

At nine o'clock that evening, a ragged, unshorn man, with the look of one not well at ease with the world, crept up the little plantation. He had a sack on his back for his ill-gotten plunder, and a mighty stick in case of a chance encounter. He visited his traps, hidden away in little nooks, where no man might find them, and it would have seemed as if trade were brisk, for his sack was heavy, and his air was cheerful. He looked out from behind the dyke at his last snare carefully, as behoved one in danger; and then with a start he crouched, for he saw the figure of a man.

There was no doubt about it; it was his bitterest enemy, the keeper of Cademuir. He made as if to crawl away, when by chance he looked again. The man lay very still. A minute later he had rushed forward with a white face, and was working as if for his life.

In half an hour two men might have been seen in that little glen. One, with a grey, sickened face, was gazing vacantly around him, with the look of someone awakened from a long sleep. By dint of much toil, and half a bottle of brandy, he had been brought back from what was like to have been the longest sleep he had ever taken. Beside him on the grass, with wild eyes, sat the poacher, shedding hysterical tears. "Dae onything ye like wi' me," he was saying, "kick me or kill me, an' I'm ready. I'll gang to jail wi' ye, to Peebles or the Calton, an' no say a word. But oh—! ma God, I thocht ye were bye wi't."

AT THE RISING OF THE WATERS

In mid-September the moors are changing from red to a dusky brown, as the fire of the heather wanes, and the long grass yellows with advancing autumn. Then, too, the rain falls heavily on the hills, and vexes the shallow upland streams, till every glen is ribbed with its churning torrent. This for the uplands; but below, at the rim of the plains, where the glens expand to vales, and trim fields edge the wastes, there is wreck and lamentation. The cabined waters lip over cornland and meadow, and bear destruction to crop and cattle.

This is the tale of Robert Linklater, farmer in Clachlands, and the events which befell him on the night of September 20th, in the year of grace 1880. I am aware that there are characters in the countryside which stand higher in repute than his, for imagination and a love of point and completeness in a story are qualities which little commend themselves to the prosaic. I have heard him called "Leein' Rob," and answer to the same with cheerfulness; but he was wont in private to brag of minutest truthfulness, and attribute his ill name to the universal dullness of man.

On this evening he came home, by his own account, from market about the hour of six. He had had a week of festivity. On the Monday he had gone to a distant cattle-show, and on

Tuesday to a marriage. On the Wednesday he had attended upon a cousin's funeral, and, being flown with whisky, brought everlasting disgrace upon himself by rising to propose the health of the bride and bridegroom. On Thursday he had been at the market of Gledsmuir, and, getting two shillings more for his ewes than he had reckoned, returned in a fine fervour of spirit and ripe hilarity.

The weather had been shower and blast for days. The grey skies dissolved in dreary rain, and on that very morn there had come a downpour so fierce that the highways ran like a hillside torrent. Now, as he sat at supper and looked down at the green vale and red waters leaping by bank and brae, a sudden fear came to his heart. Hitherto he had had no concern—for was not his harvest safely inned? But now he minds of the laigh parks and the nowt beasts there, which he had bought the week before at the sale of Inverforth. They were Kyloe and Galloway mixed, and on them, when fattened through winter and spring, lay great hopes of profit. He gulped his meal down hurriedly, and went forthwith to the garden foot. There he saw something that did not allay his fears. Gled had split itself in two, at the place where Clachlands water came to swell its flow, and a long, gleaming line of black current stole round by the side of the laigh meadow, where stood the huddled cattle. Let but the waters rise a little, and the valley would be one uniform, turgid sea.

This was pleasing news for an honest man after a hard day's work, and the farmer went grumbling back. He took a mighty plaid and flung it over his shoulders, chose the largest and toughest of his many sticks, and set off to see wherein he could better the peril.

Now, some hundreds of yards above the laigh meadow, a crazy wooden bridge spanned the stream. By this way he might bring his beasts to safety, for no nowt could hope to swim the red flood. So he plashed through the dripping stubble to the river's brink, where, with tawny swirl, it licked the edge of banks which in summer weather stood high and flower-decked. Ruefully he reflected that many good palings would by this time be whirling to a distant sea.

When he came to the wooden bridge he set his teeth manfully and crossed. It creaked and swayed with his weight, and dipped till it all but touched the flow. It could not stand even as the water was, for already its mid prop had lurched forward, like a drunken man, and was groaning at each wave. But if a rise came, it would be torn from its foundations like a reed, and then heigh-ho! for cattle and man.

With painful haste he laboured through the shallows which rimmed the haughlands, and came to the snake-like current which had even now spread itself beyond the laigh meadow. He measured its depth with his eye and ventured. It did not reach beyond his middle, but its force gave him much ado to keep his feet. At length it was passed, and he stood triumphant on the spongy land, where the cattle huddled in mute discomfort and terror.

Darkness was falling, and he could scarcely see the homestead on the affronting hillside. So with all speed he set about collecting the shivering beasts, and forcing them through the ring of water to the bridge. Up to their flanks they went, and then stood lowing helplessly. He saw that something was wrong, and made to ford the current himself. But now it was beyond him. He looked down at the yellow water running round his middle, and saw that it had risen, and was rising inch by inch with every minute. Then he glanced to where aforetime stood the crazy planking of the bridge. Suddenly hope and complacency fled, and the gravest fear settled in his heart; for he saw no bridge, only a ragged, saw-like end of timber where once he had crossed.

Here was a plight for a solitary man to be in at nightfall. There would be no wooden bridge on all the water, and the nearest one of stone was at distant Gledsmuir, over some score of miles of weary moorland. It was clear that his cattle must bide on this farther bank, and he himself, when once he had seen them in safety, would set off for the nearest farm and pass the night. It seemed the craziest of matters, that he should be thus in peril and discomfort, with the lights of his house blinking not a quarter mile away.

Once more he tried to break the water-ring and once more he failed. The flood was still rising, and the space of green which showed grey and black beneath a fitful moon was quickly lessening. Before, irritation had been his upper feeling, now terror succeeded. He could not swim a stroke, and if the field were covered he would drown like a cat in a bag. He lifted up his voice and roared with all the strength of his mighty lungs, "Sammle," "Andra," "Jock," "come and help's," till the place rang with echoes. Meantime, with strained eyes he watched the rise of the cruel water, which crept, black and pitiless, over the shadowy grey.

He drove the beasts to a little knoll, which stood somewhat above the meadow, and there they stood, cattle and man, in the fellowship of misfortune. They had been as wild as peat-reek, and had suffered none to approach them, but now with some instinct of peril they stood quietly by his side, turning great billowy foreheads to the surging waste. Upward and nearer came the current, rising with steady gurgling which told of great storms in his hills and roaring torrents in every gorge. Now the sound grew louder and seemed almost at his feet, now it ceased and nought was heard save the dull hum of the main stream pouring its choking floods to the sea. Suddenly his eyes wandered to the lights of his house and the wide slope beyond, and for a second he mused on some alien trifle. Then he was brought to himself with a pull as he looked and saw a line of black water not three feet from the farthest beast. His heart stood still, and with awe he reflected that in half-an-hour by this rate of rising he would be with his Maker.

For five minutes he waited, scarce daring to look around him, but dreading each instant to feel a cold wave lick his boot. Then he glanced timorously, and to his joy it was scarce an inch higher. It was stopping, and he might yet be safe. With renewed energy he cried out for aid, till the very cattle started at the sound and moved uneasily among themselves.

In a little there came an answering voice across the dark, "Whae's in the laigh meedy?" and it was the voice of the herd of Clachlands, sounding hoarse through the driving of the stream.

"It's me," went back the mournful response.

"And whae are ye?" came the sepulchral voice.

"Your ain maister, William Smail, forewandered among water and nowt beast."

For some time there was no reply, since the shepherd was engaged in a severe mental struggle; with the readiness of his class he went straight to the heart of the peril, and mentally reviewed the ways and waters of the land. Then he calmly accepted the hopelessness of it all, and cried loudly through the void,—

"There's nae way for't but juist to bide where ye are. The water's stoppit, and gin mornin' we'll get ye aff. I'll send a laddie down to the Dow Pule to bring up a boat in a cairt. But that's a lang gait, and it'll be a sair job gettin' it up, and I misdoot it'll be daylicht or he comes. But haud up your hert, and we'll get ye oot. Are the beasts a' richt?"

"A' richt, William; but, 'od man! their maister is cauld. Could ye no fling something ower?"

"No, when there's twae hunner yairds o' deep water atween."

"Then, William, ye maun licht a fire, a great muckle roarin' fire, juist fornenst me. It'll cheer me to see the licht o' 't."

The shepherd did as he was bid, and for many minutes the farmer could hear the noise of men heaping wood, in the pauses of wind and through the thicker murmur of the water. Then a glare shot up, and revealed the dusky forms of the four serving-men straining their eyes across the channel. The gleam lit up a yard of water by the other bank, but all midway was inky shadow. It was about eight o'clock, and the moon was just arisen. The air had coldened and a light chill wind rose from the river.

The farmer of Clachlands, standing among shivering and dripping oxen, himself wet to the skin and cold as a stone, with no wrapping save his plaid, and no outlook save a black moving water and a gleam of fire—in such a position, the farmer of Clachlands collected his thoughts and mustered his resolution. His first consideration was the safety of his stock. The effort gave him comfort. His crops were in, and he could lose nothing there; his sheep were far removed from scaith, and his cattle would survive the night with ease, if the water kept its level. With some satisfaction he reflected that the only care he need have in the matter was for his own bodily comfort in an autumn night. This was serious, yet not deadly, for the farmer was a man of many toils and cared little for the rigours of weather. But he would gladly have given the price of a beast for a bottle of whisky to comfort himself in this emergency.

He stood on a knuckle of green land some twenty feet long, with a crowd of cattle pressing around him and a little forest of horns showing faintly. There was warmth in these great shaggy hides if they had not been drenched and icy from long standing. His fingers were soon as numb as his feet, and it was in vain that he stamped on the plashy grass or wrapped his hands in a fold of plaid. There was no doubt in the matter. He was keenly uncomfortable, and the growing chill of night would not mend his condition.

Some ray of comfort was to be got from the sight of the crackling fire. There at least was homely warmth, and light, and ease. With gusto he conjured up all the delights of the past week, the roaring evenings in market ale-house, and the fragrance of good drink and piping food. Necessity sharpened his fancy, and he could almost feel the flavour of tobacco. A sudden hope took him. He clapped hand to pocket and pulled forth pipe and shag. Curse it! He had left his match-box on the chimney-top in his kitchen, and there was an end to his only chance of comfort.

So in all cold and damp he set himself to pass the night in the midst of that ceaseless swirl of black moss water. Even as he looked at the dancing glimmer of fire, the moon broke forth silent and full, and lit the vale with misty glamour. The great hills, whence came the Gled, shone blue and high with fleecy trails of vapour drifting athwart them. He saw clearly the walls of his dwelling, the light shining from the window, the struggling fire on the bank, and the dark forms of men. Its transient flashes on the waves were scarce seen in the broad belt of moonshine which girdled the valley. And around him, before and behind, rolled the unending desert waters with that heavy, resolute flow, which one who knows the floods fears a thousandfold more than the boisterous stir of a torrent.

And so he stood till maybe one o'clock of the morning, cold to the bone, and awed by the eternal silence, which choked him, despite the myriad noises of the night. For there are few things more awful than the calm of nature in her madness—the stillness which follows a snow-slip or the monotony of a great flood. By this hour he was falling from his first high confidence. His knees stooped under him, and he was fain to lean upon the beasts at his side. His shoulders ached with the wet, and his eyes grew sore with the sight of yellow glare and remote distance.

From this point I shall tell his tale in his own words, as he has told it me, but stripped of its garnishing and detail. For it were vain to translate Lallan into orthodox speech, when the very salt of the night air clings to the Scots as it did to that queer tale.

"The mune had been lang out," he said, "and I had grown weary o' her blinkin'. I was as cauld as death, and as wat as the sea, no to speak o' haein' the rheumatics in my back. The nowt were glowrin' and glunchin', rubbin' heid to heid, and whiles stampin' on my taes wi' their cloven hooves. But I was mortal glad o' the beasts' company, for I think I wad hae gane daft mysel in that muckle dowie water. Whiles I thocht it was risin', and then my hert stood still; an' whiles fa'in', and then it loupit wi' joy. But it keepit geyan near the bit, and aye as I heard it lip-lappin' I prayed the Lord to keep it whaur it was.

"About half-past yin in the mornin', as I saw by my watch, I got sleepy, and but for the nowt steerin', I micht hae drappit aff. Syne I begood to watch the water, and it was rale interestin', for a' sort o' queer things were comin' doun. I could see bits o' brigs and palin's wi'oot end dippin' in the tide, and whiles swirlin' in sae near that I could hae grippit them. Then beasts began to come by, whiles upside doun, whiles soomin' brawly, sheep and stirks frae the farms up the water. I got graund amusement for a wee while watchin' them, and notin' the marks on their necks.

"'That's Clachlands Mains,' says I, 'and that's Nether Fallo, and the Back o' the Muneraw. Gudesake, sic a spate it maun hae been up the muirs to work siccan a destruction!' I keepit coont o' the stock, and feegured to mysel what the farmer-bodies wad lose. The thocht that I wad keep a' my ain was some kind o' comfort.

"But about the hour o' twae the mune cloudit ower, and I saw nae mair than twenty feet afore me. I got awesome cauld, and a sort o' stound o' fricht took me, as I lookit into that black, unholy water. The nowt shivered sair and drappit their heids, and the fire on the ither side seemed to gang out a' of a sudden, and leave the hale glen thick wi' nicht. I shivered mysel wi' something mair than the snell air, and there and then I wad hae gien the price o' fower stirks for my ain bed at hame.

"It was as quiet as a kirkyaird, for suddenly the roar o' the water stoppit, and the stream lay still as a loch. Then I heard a queer lappin' as o' something floatin' doun, and it sounded miles aff in that dreidfu' silence. I listened wi' een stertin', and aye it cam' nearer and nearer, wi' a sound like a dowg soomin' a burn. It was sae black, I could see nocht, but somewhere frae the edge o' a cloud, a thin ray o' licht drappit on the water, and there, soomin' doun by me, I saw something that lookit like a man.

"My hert was burstin' wi' terror, but, thinks I, here's a droonin' body, and I maun try and save it. So I waded in as far as I daured, though my feet were sae cauld that they bowed aneath me.

"Ahint me I heard a splashin' and fechtin', and then I saw the nowt, fair wild wi' fricht, standin' in the water on the ither side o' the green bit, and lookin' wi' muckle feared een at something in the water afore me.

"Doun the thing came, and aye I got caulder as I looked. Then it was by my side, and I claught at it and pu'd it after me on to the land.

"I heard anither splash. The nowt gaed farther into the water, and stood shakin' like young birks in a storm.

"I got the thing upon the green bank and turned it ower. It was a drooned man wi' his hair hingin' back on his broo, and his mouth wide open. But first I saw his een, which glowered like scrapit lead out o' his clay-cauld face, and had in them a' the fear o' death and hell which follows after.

"The next moment I was up to my waist among the nowt, fechtin' in the water aside them, and snowkin' into their wet backs to hide mysel like a feared bairn.

"Maybe half an 'oor I stood, and then my mind returned to me. I misca'ed mysel for a fule and a coward. And my legs were sae numb, and my strength sae far gane, that I kenned fine that I couldna lang thole to stand this way like a heron in the water.

"I lookit round, and then turned again wi' a stert, for there were thae leaden een o' that awfu' deid thing staring at me still.

"For anither quarter-hour I stood and shivered, and then my guid sense returned, and I tried again. I walkit backward, never lookin' round, through the water to the shore, whaur I thocht the corp was lyin'. And a' the time I could hear my hert chokin' in my breist.

"My God, I fell ower it, and for one moment lay aside it, wi' my heid touchin' its deathly skin. Then wi' a skelloch like a daft man, I took the thing in my airms and flung it wi' a' my strength into the water. The swirl took it, and it dipped and swam like a fish till it gaed out o' sicht.

"I sat doun on the grass and grat like a bairn wi' fair horror and weakness. Yin by yin the nowt came back, and shouthered anither around me, and the puir beasts brocht me yince mair to mysel. But I keepit my een on the grund, and thocht o' hame and a' thing decent and kindly, for I daurna for my life look out to the black water in dreid o' what it micht bring.

"At the first licht, the herd and twae ither men cam' ower in a boat to tak me aff and bring fodder for the beasts. They fand me still sitting wi' my heid atween my knees, and my face like a peeled wand. They lifted me intil the boat and rowed me ower, driftin' far doun wi' the angry current. At the ither side the shepherd says to me in an awed voice,—

"'There's a fearfu' thing happened. The young laird o' Manorwater's drooned in the spate. He was ridin' back late and tried the ford o' the Cauldshaw foot. Ye ken his wild cantrips, but there's an end o' them noo. The horse cam' hame in the nicht wi' an empty saiddle, and the Gled Water rinnin' frae him in streams. The corp'll be far on to the sea by this time, and they'll never see't mair.'

"'I ken,' I cried wi' a dry throat, 'I ken; I saw him floatin' by.' And then I broke yince mair into a silly greetin', while the men watched me as if they thocht I was out o' my mind."

So much the farmer of Clachlands told me, but to the countryside he repeated merely the bare facts of weariness and discomfort. I have heard that he was accosted a week later by the minister of the place, a well-intentioned, phrasing man, who had strayed from his native city with its familiar air of tea and temperance to those stony uplands.

"And what thoughts had you, Mr Linklater, in that awful position? Had you no serious reflection upon your life?"

"Me," said the farmer; "no me. I juist was thinkin' that it was dooms cauld, and that I wad hae gien a guid deal for a pipe o' tobaccy." This in the racy, careless tone of one to whom such incidents were the merest child's play.

SKULE SKERRY

ANTHONY HURRELL'S STORY

Who's there, besides foul weather?—
        King Lear.

Mr Anthony Hurrell was a small man, thin to the point of emaciation, but erect as a ramrod and wiry as a cairn terrier. There was no grey in his hair, and his pale far-sighted eyes had the alertness of youth, but his lean face was so wrinkled by weather that in certain lights it looked almost venerable, and young men, who at first sight had imagined him their contemporary, presently dropped into the "sir" reserved for indisputable seniors. His actual age was, I believe, somewhere in the forties. He had inherited a small property in Northumberland, where he had accumulated a collection of the rarer wildfowl, but much of his life had been spent in places so remote that his friends could with difficulty find them on the map. He had written a dozen ornithological monographs, was joint editor of the chief modern treatise on British birds, and had been the first man to visit the tundras of the Yenisei. He spoke little and that with an agreeable hesitation, but his ready smile, his quick interest, and the impression he gave of having a fathomless knowledge of strange modes of life, made him a popular and intriguing figure among his friends. Of his doings in the War he told us nothing; what we knew of them—and they were sensational enough in all conscience—we learned elsewhere. It was Nightingale's story which drew him from his customary silence. At the dinner following that event he made certain comments on current explanations of the supernormal. "I remember once," he began, and before we knew he had surprised us by embarking on a tale.

He had scarcely begun before he stopped. "I'm boring you," he said deprecatingly. "There's nothing much in the story . . . You see, it all happened, so to speak, inside my head . . . I don't want to seem an egotist . . ."

"Don't be an ass, Tony," said Lamancha. "Every adventure takes place chiefly inside the head of somebody. Go on. We're all attention."

"It happened a good many years ago," Hurrell continued, "when I was quite a young man. I wasn't the cold scientist then that I fancy I am to-day. I took up birds in the first instance chiefly because they fired what imagination I possess. They fascinated me, for they seemed of all created things the nearest to pure spirit—those little beings with a normal temperature of 125°. Think of it. The goldcrest, with a stomach no bigger than a bean, flies across the North Sea! The curlew sandpiper, which breeds so far north that only about three people have ever seen its nest, goes to Tasmania for its holidays! So I always went bird-hunting with a queer sense of expectation and a bit of a tremor, as if I was walking very near the boundaries of the things we are not allowed to know. I felt this especially in the migration season. The small atoms, coming God knows whence and going God knows whither, were sheer mystery—they belonged to a world built in different dimensions from ours. I don't know what I expected, but I was always waiting for something, as much in a flutter as a girl at her first ball. You must realise that mood of mine to understand what follows.

"One year I went to the Norland Islands for the spring migration. Plenty of people do the same, but I had the notion to do something a little different. I had a theory that migrants go north and south on a fairly narrow road. They have their corridors in the air as clearly defined as a highway, and keep an inherited memory of these corridors, like the stout conservatives they are. So I didn't go to the Blue Banks or to Noop or to Hermaness or any of the obvious places, where birds might be expected to make their first landfall.

"At that time I was pretty well read in the sagas, and had taught myself Icelandic for the purpose. Now it is written in the Saga of Earl Skuli, which is part of the Jarla Saga or Saga of the Earls, that Skuli, when he was carving out his earldom in the Scots islands, had much to do with a place called the Isle of the Birds. It is mentioned repeatedly, and the saga-man has a lot to say about the amazing multitude of birds there. It couldn't have been an ordinary gullery, for the Northmen saw too many of these to think them worth mentioning. I got it into my head that it must have been one of the alighting places of the migrants, and was probably as busy a spot to-day as in the eleventh century. The saga said it was near Halmarsness, and that is on the west side of the island of Una, so to Una I decided to go. I fairly got that Isle of Birds on the brain. From the map it might be any one of a dozen skerries under the shadow of Halmarsness.

"I remember that I spent a good many hours in the British Museum before I started, hunting up the scanty records of those parts. I found—I think it was in Adam of Bremen—that a succession of holy men had lived on the isle, and that a chapel had been built there and endowed by Earl Rognvald, which came to an end in the time of Malise of Strathearn. There was a bare mention of the place, but the chronicler had one curious note. '*Insula Avium*,' ran the text, '*quæ est ultima insula et proximo Abysso.*' I wondered what on earth he meant. The place was not ultimate in any geographical sense, neither the farthest north nor the farthest west of the Norlands. And what was the 'abyss'? In monkish Latin the word generally means Hell—Bunyan's Bottomless Pit—and sometimes the grave; but neither meaning seemed to have much to do with an ordinary sea skerry.

"I arrived at Una about eight o'clock in a May evening, having been put across from Voss in a flit-boat. It was a quiet evening, the sky without clouds but so pale as to be almost grey, the sea grey also but with a certain iridescence in it, and the low lines of the land a combination of hard greys and umbers, cut into by the harder white of the lighthouse. I can never find words to describe that curious quality of light that you get up in the North. Sometimes it is like looking at the world out of deep water—Farquharson used to call it 'milky,' and one saw what he meant. Generally it is a sort of essence of light, cold and pure and distilled, as if it were reflected from snow. There is no colour in it, and it makes thin shadows. Some people find it horribly depressing—Farquharson said it reminded him of a churchyard in the early morning where all his friends were buried—but personally I found it tonic and comforting. But it made me feel very near the edge of the world.

"There was no inn, so I put up at the post-office, which was on a causeway between a freshwater loch and a sea voe, so that from the doorstep you could catch brown trout on one side and sea-trout on the other. Next morning I set off for Halmarsness, which lay five miles to the west over a flat moorland all puddled with tiny lochans. There seemed to be nearly as much water as land. Presently I came to a bigger loch under the lift of ground which was Halmarsness. There was a gap in the ridge through which I looked straight out to the Atlantic, and there in the middle distance was what I knew instinctively to be my island.

"It was perhaps a quarter of a mile long, low for the most part, but rising in the north to a grassy knoll beyond the reach of any tides. In parts it narrowed to a few yards' width, and the lower levels must often have been awash. But it was an island, not a reef, and I thought I could make out the remains of the monkish cell. I climbed Halmarsness, and there, with nesting skuas swooping angrily about my head, I got a better view. It was certainly my island, for the rest of the archipelago were inconsiderable skerries, and I realised that it might well be a resting-place for migrants, for the mainland cliffs were too thronged with piratical skuas and other jealous fowl to be comfortable for weary travellers.

"I sat for a long time on the headland looking down from the three hundred feet of basalt to the island half a mile off—the last bit of solid earth between me and Greenland. The sea was calm for Norland waters, but there was a snowy edging of surf to the skerries which told of a tide rip. Two miles farther south I could see the entrance to the famous Roost of Una, where, when tide and wind collide, there is a wall like a house, so that a small steamer cannot pass it. The only sign of human habitation was a little grey farm in the lowlands toward the Roost, but the place was full of the evidence of man—a herd of Norland ponies, each tagged with its owner's name—grazing sheep of the piebald Norland breed—a broken barbed-wire fence that drooped over the edge of the cliff. I was only an hour's walk from a telegraph office, and a village which got its newspapers not more than three days late. It was a fine spring noon, and in the empty bright land there was scarcely a shadow . . . All the same, as I looked down at the island I did not wonder that it had been selected for attention by the saga-man and had been reputed holy. For it had an air of concealing something, though it was as bare as a billiard-table. It was an intruder, an irrelevance in the picture, planted there by some celestial caprice. I decided forthwith to make my camp on it, and the decision, inconsequently enough, seemed to me to be something of a venture.

"That was the view taken by John Ronaldson, when I talked to him after dinner. John was the post-mistress's son, more fisherman than crofter, like all Norlanders, a skilful sailor and an adept at the dipping lug, and noted for his knowledge of the western coast. He had difficulty in understanding my plan, and when he identified my island he protested.

"'Not Skule Skerry!' he cried. 'What would take ye there, man? Ye'll get a' the birds ye want on Halmarsness and a far better bield. Ye'll be blawn away on the skerry, if the wund rises.'

"I explained to him my reasons as well as I could, and I answered his fears about a gale by pointing out that the island was sheltered by the cliffs from the prevailing winds, and could be scourged only from the south, south-west, or west, quarters from which the wind rarely blew in May. 'It'll be cauld,' he said, 'and wat.' I pointed out that I had a tent and was accustomed to camping. 'Ye'll starve'—I expounded my proposed methods of commissariat. 'It'll be an ill job getting ye on and off'—but after cross-examination he admitted that ordinarily the tides were not difficult, and that I could get a row-boat to a beach below the farm I had seen—its name was Sgurravoe. Yet when I had said all this he still raised objections, till I asked him flatly what was the matter with Skule Skerry.

"'Naebody gangs there,' he said gruffly.

"'Why should they?' I asked. 'I'm only going to watch the birds.'

"But the fact that it was never visited seemed to stick in his throat and he grumbled out something that surprised me. 'It has an ill name,' he said. But when I pressed him he admitted that there was no record of shipwreck or disaster to account for the ill name. He repeated the words 'Skule Skerry' as if they displeased him. 'Folk dinna gang near it. It has aye had an ill name. My grandfather used to say that the place wasna canny.'

"Now your Norlander has nothing of the Celt in him, and is as different from the Hebridean as a Northumbrian from a Cornishman. They are a fine, upstanding, hard-headed race, almost pure Scandinavian in blood, but they have as little poetry in them as a Manchester radical. I should have put them down as utterly free from superstition, and, in all my many visits to the islands I have never yet come across a folk-tale—hardly even a historical legend. Yet here was John Ronaldson, with his weather-beaten face and stiff chin and shrewd blue eyes, declaring that an innocent-looking island 'wasna canny,' and showing the most remarkable disinclination to go near it.

"Of course all this only made me keener. Besides, it was called Skule Skerry, and the name could only come from Earl Skuli; so it was linked up authentically with the oddments of information I had collected in the British Museum—the Jarla Saga and Adam of Bremen and all the rest of it. John finally agreed to take me over next morning in his boat, and I spent the rest of the day in collecting my kit. I had a small E.P. tent, and a Wolseley valise and half a dozen rugs, and, since I had brought a big box of tinned stuffs from the Stores, all I needed was flour and meal and some simple groceries. I learned that there was a well on the island, and that I could count on sufficient driftwood for my fire, but to make certain I took a sack of coals and another of peats. So I set off next day in John's boat, ran with the wind through the Roost of Una when the tide was right, tacked up the coast, and came to the skerry early in the afternoon.

"You could see that John hated the place. We ran into a cove on the east side, and he splashed ashore as if he expected to have his landing opposed, looking all the time sharply about him. When he carried my stuff to a hollow under the knoll which gave a certain amount of shelter, his head was always twisting round. To me the place seemed to be the last word in forgotten peace. The swell lipped gently on the reefs and the little pebbled beaches, and only the babble of gulls from Halmarsness broke the stillness.

"John was clearly anxious to get away, but he did his duty by me. He helped me to get the tent up, found a convenient place for my boxes, pointed out the well and filled my water bucket, and made a zareba of stones to protect my camp on the Atlantic side. We had brought a small dinghy along with us, and this was to be left with me, so that when I wanted I could row across to the beach at Sgurravoe. As his last service he fixed an old pail between two boulders on the summit of the knoll, and filled it with oily waste, so that it could be turned into a beacon.

"'Ye'll maybe want to come off,' he said, 'and the boat will maybe no be there. Kindle your flare, and they'll see it at Sgurravoe and get the word to me, and I'll come for ye though the Muckle Black Silkie himsel' was hunkerin' on the skerry.'

"Then he looked up and sniffed the air. 'I dinna like the set of the sky,' he declared. 'It's a bad weatherhead. There'll be mair wund than I like in the next four and twenty hours.'

"So saying, he hoisted his sail and presently was a speck on the water towards the Roost. There was no need for him to hurry, for the tide was now wrong, and before he could pass the Roost he would have three hours to wait on this side of the Mull. But the man, usually so deliberate and imperturbable, had been in a fever to be gone.

"His departure left me in a curious mood of happy loneliness and pleasurable expectation. I was left solitary with the seas and the birds. I laughed to think that I had found a streak of superstition in the granite John. He and his Muckle Black Silkie! I knew the old legend of the North which tells how the Finns, the ghouls that live in the deeps of the ocean, can on occasion don a seal's skin and come to land to play havoc with mortals. But diablerie and this isle of mine were worlds apart. I looked at it as the sun dropped, drowsing in the opal-coloured tides, under a sky in which pale clouds made streamers like a spectral aurora borealis, and I thought that I had stumbled upon one of those places where Nature seems to invite one to her secrets. As the light died the sky was flecked as with the roots and branches of some great nebular tree. That would be the 'weatherhead' of which John Ronaldson had spoken.

"I set my fire going, cooked my supper, and made everything snug for the night. I had been right in my guess about the migrants. It must have been about ten o'clock when they began to arrive—after my fire had died out and I was smoking my last pipe before getting into my sleeping-bag. A host of fieldfares settled gently on the south part of the skerry. A faint light lingered till after midnight, but it was not easy to distinguish the little creatures, for they were aware of my presence and did not alight within a dozen yards of me. But I made out bramblings and buntings and what I thought was the Greenland wheatear; also jack snipe and sanderling; and I believed from their cries that the curlew sandpiper and the whimbrel were there. I went to sleep in a state of high excitement, promising myself a fruitful time on the morrow.

"I slept badly, as one often does one's first night in the open. Several times I woke with a start under the impression that I was in a boat rowing swiftly with the tide. And every time I woke I heard the flutter of myriad birds, as if a velvet curtain was being slowly switched along an oak floor. At last I fell into deeper sleep, and when I opened my eyes it was full day.

"The first thing that struck me was that it had got suddenly colder. The sky was stormily red in the east, and masses of woolly clouds were banking in the north. I lit my fire with numbed fingers and hastily made tea. I could see the nimbus of seafowl over Halmarsness, but there was only one bird left on my skerry. I was certain from its forked tail that it was a Sabine's gull, but before I got my glass out it was disappearing into the haze towards the north. The sight cheered and excited me, and I cooked my breakfast in pretty good spirits.

"That was literally the last bird that came near me, barring the ordinary shearwaters and gulls and cormorants that nested round about Halmarsness. (There was not one single nest of any sort on the island. I had heard of that happening before in places which were regular halting grounds for migrants.) The travellers must have had an inkling of the coming weather and were waiting somewhere well to the south. For about nine o'clock it began to blow. Great God, how it blew! You must go to the Norlands if you want to know what wind can be. It is like being on a mountain-top, for there is no high ground to act as a wind-break. There was no rain, but the surf broke in showers and every foot of the skerry was drenched with it. In a trice Halmarsness was hidden, and I seemed to be in the centre of a maelstrom, choked with scud and buffeted on every side by swirling waters.

"Down came my tent at once. I wrestled with the crazy canvas and got a black eye from a pole, but I managed to drag the ruins into the shelter of the zareba which John had built, and tumble some of the bigger boulders on it. There it lay, flapping like a sick albatross. The water got into my food boxes, and soaked my fuel, as well as every inch of my clothing . . . I had looked forward to a peaceful day of watching and meditation, when I could write up my notes; and instead I spent a morning like a Rugger scrum. I might have enjoyed it, if I hadn't been so wet and cold, and could have got a better lunch than some clammy mouthfuls out of a tin. One talks glibly about being 'blown off' a place, generally an idle exaggeration—but that day I came very near the reality. There were times when I had to hang on for dear life to one of the bigger stones to avoid being trundled into the yeasty seas.

"About two o'clock the volume of the storm began to decline, and then for the first time I thought about the boat. With a horrid sinking of the heart I scrambled to the cove where we had beached it. It had been drawn up high and dry, and its painter secured to a substantial boulder. But now there was not a sign of it except a ragged rope-end round the stone. The tide had mounted to its level, and tide and wind had smashed the rotten painter. By this time what was left of it would be tossing in the Roost.

"This was a pretty state of affairs. John was due to visit me next day, but I had a cold twenty-four hours ahead of me. There was of course the flare he had left me, but I was not inclined to use this. It looked like throwing up the sponge and confessing that my expedition had been a farce. I felt miserable, but obstinate, and, since the weather was clearly mending, I determined to put the best face on the business, so I went back to the wreckage of my camp, and tried to tidy up. There was still far too much wind to do anything with the tent, but the worst of the spindrift had ceased, and I was able to put out my bedding and some of my provender to dry. I got a dry jersey out of my pack, and, as I was wearing fisherman's boots and oilskins, I managed to get some slight return of comfort. Also at last I succeeded in lighting a pipe. I found a corner under the knoll which gave me a modicum of shelter, and I settled myself to pass the time with tobacco and my own thoughts.

"About three o'clock the wind died away completely. That I did not like, for a dead lull in the Norlands is often the precursor of a new gale. Indeed, I never remembered a time when some wind did not blow, and I had heard that when such a thing happened people came out of their houses to ask what the matter was. But now we had the deadest sort of calm. The sea was still wild and broken, the tides raced by like a mill-stream, and a brume was gathering which shut out Halmarsness—shut out every prospect except a narrow circuit of grey water. The cessation of the racket of the gale made the place seem uncannily quiet. The present tumult of the sea, in comparison with the noise of the morning, seemed no more than a mutter and an echo.

"As I sat there I became conscious of an odd sensation. I seemed to be more alone, more cut off, not only from my fellows but from the habitable earth, than I had ever been before. It was like being in a small boat in mid-Atlantic—but worse, if you understand me, for that would have been loneliness in the midst of a waste which was nevertheless surrounded and traversed by the works of man, whereas now I felt that I was clean outside man's ken. I had come somehow to the edge of that world where life is, and was very close to the world which has only death in it.

"At first I do not think there was much fear in the sensation—chiefly strangeness, but the kind of strangeness which awes without exciting. I tried to shake off the mood, and got up to stretch myself. There was not much room for exercise, and as I moved with stiff legs along the reefs I slipped into the water, so that I got my arms wet. It was cold beyond belief—the very quintessence of deathly Arctic ice, so cold that it seemed to sear and bleach the skin.

"From that moment I date the most unpleasant experience of my life. I became suddenly the prey of a black depression, shot with the red lights of terror. But it was not a numb terror, for my brain was acutely alive . . . I had the sense to try to make tea, but my fuel was still too damp, and the best I could do was to pour half the contents of my brandy flask into a cup and swallow the stuff. That did not properly warm my chilled body, but—since I am a very temperate man—it speeded up my thoughts instead of calming them. I felt myself on the brink of a childish panic.

"One thing I thought I saw clearly—the meaning of Skule Skerry. By some alchemy of nature, at which I could only guess, it was on the track by which the North exercised its spell, a cableway for the magnetism of that cruel frozen Uttermost, which man might penetrate but could never subdue or understand. Though the latitude was only 61°, there were folds of tucks in space, and this isle was the edge of the world. Birds knew it, and the old Northmen, who were primitive beings like the birds, knew it. That was why an inconsiderable skerry had been given the name of a conquering Jarl. The old Church knew it, and had planted a chapel to exorcise the demons of darkness. I wondered what sights the hermit, whose cell had been on the very spot where I was cowering, had seen in the winter dusks.

"It may have been partly the brandy acting on an empty stomach, and partly the extreme cold, but my brain, in spite of my efforts to think rationally, began to run like a dynamo. It is difficult to explain my mood, but I seemed to be two persons—one a reasonable modern man trying to keep sane and scornfully rejecting the fancies which the other, a cast-back to something elemental, was furiously spinning. But it was the second that had the upper hand . . . I felt myself loosed from my moorings, a mere waif on uncharted seas. What is the German phrase? *Urdummheit*—Primal Idiocy? That is what was the matter with me. I had fallen out of civilisation into the Outlands and was feeling their spell . . . I could not think, but I could remember, and what I had read of the Norse voyagers came back to me with horrid persistence. They had known the outland terrors—the Sea Walls at the world's end, the Curdled Ocean with its strange beasts. Those men did not sail north as we did, in steamers, with modern food and modern instruments, huddled into crews and expeditions. They had gone out almost alone, in brittle galleys, and they had known what we could never know.

"And then, I had a shattering revelation. I had been groping for a word and I suddenly got it. It was Adam of Bremen's '*proxima Abysso.*' This island was next door to the Abyss, and the Abyss was that blanched world of the North which was the negation of life.

"That unfortunate recollection was the last straw. I remember that I forced myself to get up and try again to kindle a fire. But the wood was still too damp, and I realised with consternation that I had very few matches left, several boxes having been ruined that morning. As I staggered about I saw the flare which John had left for me, and had almost lit it. But some dregs of manhood prevented me—I could not own defeat in that babyish way—I must wait till John Ronaldson came for me next morning. Instead I had another mouthful of brandy, and tried to eat some of my sodden biscuits. But I could scarcely swallow; this infernal cold, instead of rousing hunger, had given me only a raging thirst.

"I forced myself to sit down again with my face to the land. You see, every moment I was becoming more childish. I had the notion—I cannot call it a thought—that down the avenue from the North something terrible and strange might come. My nervous state must have been pretty bad, for though I was cold and empty and weary I was scarcely conscious of physical discomfort. My heart was fluttering like a scared boy's; and all the time the other part of me was standing aside and telling me not to be a damned fool . . . I think that if I had heard the rustle of a flock of migrants I might have pulled myself together, but not a blessed bird had come near me all day. I had fallen into a world that killed life, a sort of Valley of the Shadow of Death.

"The brume spoiled the long northern twilight, and presently it was almost dark. At first I thought that this was going to help me, and I got hold of several of my half-dry rugs, and made a sleeping-place. But I could not sleep, even if my teeth had stopped chattering, for a new and perfectly idiotic idea possessed me. It came from a recollection of John Ronaldson's parting words. What had he said about the Black Silkie—the Finn who came out of the deep and hunkered on this skerry? Raving mania! But on this lost island in the darkening night, with icy tides lapping about me, was any horror beyond belief?

"Still, the sheer idiocy of the idea compelled a reaction. I took hold of my wits with both hands and cursed myself for a fool. I could even reason about my folly. I knew what was wrong with me. I was suffering from panic—a physical affection produced by natural causes, explicable, though as yet not fully explained. Two friends of mine had once been afflicted with it; one in a lonely glen in the Jotunheim, so that he ran for ten miles over stony hills till he found a saeter and human companionship: the other in a Bavarian forest, where both he and his guide tore for hours through the thicket till they dropped like logs beside a highroad. This reflection enabled me to take a pull on myself and to think a little ahead. If my troubles were physical then there would be no shame in looking for the speediest cure. Without further delay I must leave this God-forgotten place.

"The flare was all right, for it had been set on the highest point of the island, and John had covered it with a peat. With one of my few remaining matches I lit the oily waste, and a great smoky flame leapt to heaven.

"If the half-dark had been eery, this sudden brightness was eerier. For a moment the glare gave me confidence, but as I looked at the circle of moving water evilly lit up all my terrors returned . . . How long would it take John to reach me? They would see it at once at Sgurravoe—they would be on the look-out for it—John would not waste time, for he had tried to dissuade me from coming—an hour—two hours at the most . . .

"I found I could not take my eyes from the waters. They seemed to flow from the north in a strong stream, black as the heart of the elder ice, irresistible as fate, cruel as hell. There seemed to be uncouth shapes swimming in them, which were more than the flickering shadows from the flare . . . Something portentous might at any moment come down that river of death . . . Someone . . .

"And then my knees gave under me and my heart shrank like a pea, for I saw that the someone had come.

"He drew himself heavily out of the sea, wallowed for a second, and then raised his head and, from a distance of five yards, looked me blindly in the face. The flare was fast dying down, but even so at that short range it cast a strong light, and the eyes of the awful being seemed to be dazed by it. I saw a great dark head like a bull's—an old face wrinkled as if in pain—a gleam of enormous broken teeth—a dripping beard—all formed on other lines than God has made mortal creatures. And on the right of the throat was a huge scarlet gash. The thing seemed to be moaning, and then from it came a sound—whether of anguish or wrath I cannot tell—but it seemed to be the cry of a tortured fiend.

"That was enough for me. I pitched forward in a swoon, hitting my head on a stone, and in that condition three hours later John Ronaldson found me.

"They put me to bed at Sgurravoe with hot earthenware bottles, and the doctor from Voss next day patched up my head and gave me a sleeping draught. He declared that there was little the matter with me except shock from exposure, and promised to set me on my feet in a week.

"For three days I was as miserable as a man could be, and did my best to work myself into a fever. I had said not a word about my experience, and left my rescuers to believe that my only troubles were cold and hunger, and that I had lit the flare because I had lost the boat. But during these days I was in a critical state. I knew that there was nothing wrong with my body, but I was gravely concerned about my mind.

"For this was my difficulty. If that awful thing was a mere figment of my brain then I had better be certified at once as a lunatic. No sane man could get into such a state as to see such portents with the certainty with which I had seen that creature come out of the night. If, on the other hand, the thing was a real presence, then I had looked on something outside natural law, and my intellectual world was broken in pieces. I was a scientist, and a scientist cannot admit the supernatural. If with my eyes I had beheld the monster in which Adam of Bremen believed, which holy men had exorcised, which even the shrewd Norlanders shuddered at as the Black Silkie, then I must burn my books and revise my creed. I might take to poetry or theosophy, but I would never be much good again at science.

"On the third afternoon I was trying to doze, and with shut eyes fighting off the pictures which tormented my brain. John Ronaldson and the farmer of Sgurravoe were talking at the kitchen door. The latter asked some question, and John replied—

"'Aye, it was a wall-ross and nae mistake. It cam ashore at Gloop Ness and Sandy Fraser hae gotten the skin of it. It was deid when he found it, but no long deid. The puir beast would drift south on some floe, and it was sair hurt, for Sandy said it had a hole in its throat ye could put your nieve in. There hasna been a wall-ross come to Una since my grandfather's day.'

"I turned my face to the wall and composed myself to sleep. For now I knew that I was sane, and need not forswear science."

GLOSSARY

THE HERD OF STANDLAN

hags (p. 1) – marshy, boggy moorland
birks (p. 1) – birches
Herd (p. 2) – shepherd
callant (p. 2) – boy, young man
haughs (p. 3) – level ground by a stream or river
nowt beast (p. 3) – cattle
faulds (p. 4) – section of farm manured by sheep in folds
sheep-mawks (p. 4) – sheep-maggots
pipe-stapples (p. 4) – stem of a clay pipe
wanchancy (p. 4) – dangerous, unlucky
whaups (p. 6) – curlews
thole (p. 6) – suffer, endure
as deid's a peery (p. 6) – as dead as a stone
stelled-like (p. 7) – fixed, staring
groo (p. 7) – shudder
mutch (p. 8) – a woman's cap
no canny (p. 8) – not natural
the Buik (p. 9) – the Book (i.e. the Bible)
black-avised man (p. 10) – a man with a dark, swarthy complexion
pyet (p. 11) – magpie

gyte (p. 12) – demented
soomin' (p. 13) – swimming
fleech (p. 13) – beg, implore
fair wud wi' terror (p. 13) – mad with fright
skellochs (p. 13) – screams
hankit (p. 13) – caught, snagged
the dad he had gotten (p. 15) – the blow he had received
far ower laigh (p. 15) – too low

ON CADEMUIR HILL

"The Linton Ploughman" (p. 17) – a dance in Peeblesshire
howe (p. 18) – a hollow
"hard-handed men" (p. 20) – from *A Midsummer Night's Dream*, Act 5 scene 1
stelled (p. 20) – fixed, staring
brae face (p. 21) – the front or slope of a hill
bent (p. 21) – coarse grass
Dollar Law . . . Scrape (p. 22) – two hills near Peebles
a text from the Scriptures (p. 22) – Psalm 114, "The mountains skipped like rams, and the little hills like lambs"
Natura Benigna / Maligna (p. 22) – Nature in all its beauty / cruelty
whaups (p. 23) – curlews

AT THE RISING OF THE WATERS

nowt beasts (p. 26) – cattle
plashed – (p. 27) – splashed

GLOSSARY

haughlands (p. 27) – level ground by a stream or river
affronting (p. 27) – facing (archaic)
laigh meedy (p. 29) – low meadow
herd (p. 29) – shepherd
misdoot (p. 30) – doubt, suspect
scaith (p. 30) – loss, injury
plashy (p. 31) – sodden
shag (p. 31) – tobacco
athwart (p. 32) – across
glunchin' (p. 32) – eating noisily
dowie (p. 32) – sad, dismal
steerin' (p. 33) – stirring
begood (p. 33) – began
brigs and palin's (p. 33) – bridges and fences
soomin' (p. 33) – swimming
stirks (p. 33) – young cattle
claught (p. 34) – laid hold of
birks (p. 34) – birches
snowkin' (p. 34) – sniffing, snuffling
thole (p. 34) – suffer, endure
skelloch (p. 35) – scream
shouthered (p. 35) – shouldered
cantrips (p. 35) – frolics, mischief
dooms (p. 36) – very

SKULE SKERRY

Saga of Earl Skuli (p. 39) – Skúli Thorfinsson, Earl of Caithness (c. 924–985), mentioned in the *Orkneyinga Saga*
skerries (p. 39) – low rocky islets or reefs

Adam of Bremen (p. 40) – medieval German chronicler (c. 1050–1085)

Earl Rognvald (p. 40) – Rögnvald Kali Kolsson, Earl of Orkney (c. 1100–1158)

Malise of Strathearn (p. 40) – a number of Earls of Strathearn and Orkney were called Malise, between the twelfth and fourteenth centuries; it is not clear which one is referred to here

Insula Avium (p. 40) – Island of the Birds

quæ est ultima insula et proximo Abysso (p. 40) – which is the furthest island and nearest to the Abyss

Bunyan (p. 40) – John Bunyan (1628–1688), author of the Christian allegory *Pilgrim's Progress* (1678)

dipping lug (p. 42) – a type of four-cornered sail

bield (p. 42) – refuge, shelter

wasna canny (p. 43) – was not lucky/natural

E.P. tent (p. 44) – a British Army tent

Wolseley valise (p. 44) – a heavy waterproof canvas bedroll

zareba (p. 44) – an enclosure, or protected area (from Arabic *zaribah*, cattlepen)

weatherhead (p. 45) – coming weather

diablerie (p. 45) – devilry

Rugger (p. 47) – rugby

brume (p. 49) – mist, fog

Jotunheim (p. 52) – a mountainous area in Norway, part of the Scandinavian Mountains

nieve (p. 55) – fist